Enid Blyton

Mister Meddle's Muddles

Text illustrations by Diana Catchpole
Cover illustration by Maggie Downer

AWARD PUBLICATIONS LIMITED

Enid Blyton's Happy Days!

Snowball the Pony

Bimbo and Topsy

Run-About's Holiday

The Adventures of **Binkle and Flip**

Binkle and Flip Misbehave

Mister Meddle's Mischief

Mister Meddle's Muddles

Merry Mister Meddle

You're a Nuisance **Mister Meddle**

Collect all the titles in the series!

The Adventures of
Mr Pink-Whistle

Mr Pink-Whistle
Has Some Fun

Mr Pink-Whistle's
Party

Mr Pink-Whistle
Interferes

Hello
Mr Twiddle!

Mr Twiddle
in Trouble Again

Don't Be Silly,
Mr Twiddle!

Mr Twiddle
in Trouble Again

Shuffle
the Shoemaker

For further information on Enid Blyton please visit *www.blyton.com*

ISBN 978-1-84135-658-7

First published 1950 by George Newnes

First published by Award Publications Limited 2004
This edition first published 2010

Published by Award Publications Limited,
The Old Riding School, The Welbeck Estate,
Worksop, Nottinghamshire, S80 3LR

11 2

Printed in the United Kingdom

Contents

Chapter 1

Mister Meddle Makes a Muddle

Once, when Meddle was staying with his Aunt Jemima, he broke one of her chairs. She was very cross about it.

'Meddle, you are very careless,' she said. 'I can't imagine how you broke that chair. It was quite strong.'

'It fell over and broke itself,' said Meddle.

'Somebody must have pushed it,' said Aunt Jemima. 'Well, it's not worth mending. It's got two legs and the back broken. I must go out this morning and buy another chair. And whilst I'm about it, I may as well get another little table for the kitchen corner there. It would be useful to put trays on. And I really need a new stool for my feet. I'll go and get them straight away.'

'Shall I come with you and carry them back for you, Aunt Jemima?' asked Meddle, anxious to make up for his carelessness.

'No, thank you,' said his aunt. 'You don't suppose I want them dropped all over the road and broken before they get home, do you? I shall tell the shop to send them when their van goes out this morning. You stay here and open the door when the van comes.'

So Meddle stayed at home whilst his aunt went out. He stood at the window watching for the van to come. At last he heard a rumbling down the street and along came a heavy van. It stopped at the house next door, which was empty. Meddle tapped on the window.

'Hi!' he called. 'This is the house. Hi, deliver the goods here, please. I am waiting for them.

The man got down from the van and looked doubtfully at Meddle. 'Are you sure, sir?' he asked. 'We were told to deliver at Number 8 – and your house is 6.'

'Of course I'm sure!' said Meddle, crossly. 'I've stood here all the morning waiting for you. I'll give you a hand with the things if you like.'

'Well, my mate is here,' said the man, and he whistled to a man at the back of the van. 'This is the house,' he called. 'I'll back the van a bit and then we'll get the goods out.'

So the big van was backed a little and then the two men got to work. First they carried in a fine armchair.

'My word!' thought Meddle. 'Aunt Jemima has got a much nicer chair than the one I broke. It's a beauty. I shall like to sit and snooze in that in the evening.'

The men went back to the van and brought out a table. It was very big. Meddle stared at it in surprise. 'Well, I quite thought Aunt

Jemima would have bought a small one,' he said to himself. 'This will almost fill up the whole kitchen!'

'It's to go in the kitchen,' he told the men, and he led the way. It really did almost fill up the little room!

The men went back to the van and came out with a bed, taken to pieces. Meddle stared at it. 'Well, what's Aunt bought a bed for?' he wondered. 'She didn't say anything about a bed. I wonder where it's to go. Well, there are only two bedrooms, and hers is the bigger, so it had better go in there!'

That wasn't the end of Meddle's surprise. The men brought a sofa out of the van, some more chairs, a sideboard, some stools, some carpets, another table and heaps of pictures!

'Aunt Jemima must have gone mad!' thought Meddle, telling the men to put the things here and there. 'Yes, she must have gone quite mad! She set out to buy a chair, a little table, and a stool – and she seems to have bought a whole houseful of furniture! It's really very puzzling.'

'Well, that's the lot, sir,' said the men, and Meddle gave them five pounds. The van drove off and Meddle was left alone with all the furniture. He could really hardly move in the house, it was so crammed with chairs and tables and things!

Aunt Jemima came home at half-past twelve carrying a bag full of shopping. She let herself into the house and then stared in the greatest surprise at the hall. Usually there was a hall stand there and nothing else. But now there were two chairs, a roll of carpet, and a small table!

'Meddle!' she called. 'Meddle, what are these things doing here?'

'Well, I didn't know where you wanted them to be put, Aunt,' said Meddle. 'Just tell me, and I'll take them wherever you like!'

'Meddle, I don't want them put anywhere!' cried his aunt. 'I don't know anything about them.'

'But you bought them, didn't you?' said Meddle, in surprise. 'Aunt Jemima, do you feel all right? I must say I was rather astonished to find you had bought so much furniture this morning!'

'Are you mad, Meddle?' said his aunt, beginning to look at him in a way he didn't like at all. 'I bought what I said I'd buy this morning – a chair, a little table, and a stool.

Nothing else at all. And they can't be delivered till tomorrow. Now perhaps you will kindly tell me where all these things came from?'

'Aunt Jemima – Aunt Jemima – this is all very strange,' said Meddle, staring around at the furniture. His aunt went into the sitting-room and looked in amazement at everything there. She could hardly move.

'Meddle, what in the world have you been doing?' she said at last. 'I know you do the silliest things, but I can't think how you have managed to get all this furniture here like this, this morning. Where did it come from?'

'Two men brought it,' said Meddle. He was beginning to feel most uncomfortable.

Just then a knock came at the door. Aunt Jemima opened it. A little woman stood outside, looking rather worried.

'I'm so sorry to trouble you,' she said. 'But we are moving in next door and our furniture van hasn't come along yet. I suppose you haven't seen it, have you?'

Then Aunt Jemima guessed everything. Silly old Meddle had taken in the furniture that should have gone next door! How exactly like him! If he could meddle, he would – and his meddles always made such muddles!

'I believe a dreadful mistake has been made,' said Aunt Jemima. 'I was out this morning and my stupid nephew has taken in your furniture here.'

'Why – yes – it's my furniture!' cried the little woman, staring round the hall in surprise. 'Oh dear – and I've been waiting for it. The men are gone. Whatever shall I do?'

'Meddle shall carry it next door himself and put it wherever you want it,' said Aunt Jemima firmly. 'Meddle, do you hear me? It's no good your slinking off into the garden like that. Come back. You've made a fine old muddle and you're just going to put it right!'

'But I can't carry heavy furniture about!' cried poor Meddle, looking round at the chairs and tables in a fright.

'Well, you're going to,' said his aunt. 'Now begin right away, please, because I want to hang up my coat and hat and I can't possibly get into my bedroom until some of the things are taken from the landing!'

So poor Meddle spent the rest of the day grunting and groaning under the heavy furniture, carrying it piece by piece into the house next door. How tired he was when the evening came! He sank down into a chair and sighed heavily.

'I'm not a bit sorry for you, Meddle,' said his aunt. 'Not a bit. You just won't learn sense. You didn't use your brains this morning, so you've had to use your arms and your legs and your back, and tire them out! Perhaps next time you will use your brains and save yourself a lot of trouble.'

'I will,' said Meddle. 'I certainly will!'

But, if I know Meddle, he certainly won't!

Chapter 2

Mister Meddle Is a Snowman

One day Mister Meddle met his friend Jinks. Jinks was looking very cross, and Meddle was surprised.

'What's the matter, Jinks?' he asked.

'Someone's been taking the onions out of my garden shed,' said Jinks. 'I saw their footsteps in the snow this morning. I feel very cross.'

'You should catch the thief, Jinks,' said Meddle.

'All very well to say that, but he's gone,' said Jinks.

'Well, he may come again. Can't you hide under a bush in the garden and watch for him?' asked Meddle.

'What, sit out there in the cold every frosty

15

night, and have snow fall down my neck and the frost biting my fingers and toes? Don't be silly, Meddle,' said Jinks, and he went off with his nose in the air.

Meddle stared after him. He didn't like to be called silly. 'Oh, all right, Jinks, if you're so high and mighty I won't try to help you,' said Meddle, and he marched off too.

But on the way home a perfectly marvellous idea hopped into his head. He stopped and thought about it.

'I believe it's just the idea for catching the thief!' said Meddle. 'If I pretend to be a snowman and stand still in the middle of Jinks's front garden, I shall be able to watch and see if the robber comes in. And he won't mind me at all, because he'll think I'm only a snowman. What a wonderful idea!'

He thought about it. How could he make himself like a snowman? He didn't think it would be very pleasant to cover himself with snow on such a cold night. No – he wouldn't have snow.

'I could wear my big, new, white mackintosh cape!' thought Meddle suddenly. 'Of course! It would make me look like a snowman! What a splendid idea! And I could rub flour all over my face and make it white. And wear my own hat – snowmen always wear hats. They have sticks, too, so I can take my stick to hit the robber with.'

Meddle felt very excited. He rushed home and got out his mackintosh. It covered him almost to the ground, so it would do very well.

'How pleased Jinks will be when I catch the robber for him!' thought Meddle. 'He'll be sorry he marched off with his nose in the air!'

That night Meddle crept down the road, with his mackintosh cape rolled up under his

arm and his face white with flour. He didn't mean to put the mackintosh on until he came to Jinks's garden.

When he got there, there was no one about. So Meddle unrolled his big, white cape and put it round his shoulders.

It fell almost to his feet. He kept his hat on, and he had a scarf round his neck to keep out the cold. Snowmen often had scarves.

Well, there he stood in Jinks's front garden, dressed in white, with his hat and scarf on – and a pipe in his mouth, too, though it wasn't lit. He stood there feeling most important. Now let the robber come – and what a shock he would get!

Meddle stood there, and he stood there. It was cold. He began to shiver. He thought it would be a good idea to light his pipe. So he got out his matches, struck one and puffed at his pipe, lighting it up well.

Ah, that was better. He smoked his pipe happily – and then he suddenly heard footsteps down the road. It was the village policeman passing by.

The policeman stood by Jinks's gate and sniffed. Funny, he could smell tobacco smoke – but there was nobody about at all. Then he

caught sight of the glow in the bowl of
Meddle's pipe. Goodness! Somebody was
standing in Jinks's garden smoking – but
there was no one there except the snowman.

'How can a snowman smoke a pipe?'
wondered the policeman, puzzled. 'How
strange!'

He thought he would go into the garden
and see what could be happening. So he
opened the gate quietly and crept into the
garden.

Now Meddle had no idea it was the village
policeman. When he heard footsteps and
then heard the gate open and someone
coming inside, he at once thought it must be
the robber!

'Ah!' he thought. 'Now I'll give him a
shock!'

So he walked forward two or three steps
and yelled, 'Stop, there!'

The policeman got a dreadful shock. He
had never in his life before seen a snowman
that walked and talked. He stood still in
fright, and couldn't say a word.

The snowman walked right up to him. The
policeman simply couldn't bear it. He gave a
yell and tore out of the gate and down the

street. Meddle quite thought he must be the robber, and he tore after him, stumbling over his long, white cape.

'Help! The snowman's after me! The snowman's after me!' yelled the frightened policeman. People came running out of their houses to see what was happening, and when they saw the snowman rushing after the policeman, they were so frightened that they ran away too.

And soon Meddle found himself chasing quite a crowd of people. He began to enjoy himself. It was fun to make so many people run!

'Stop, stop!' he yelled. But nobody

stopped. They ran on and on. The policeman got to the police station. He stumbled in, panting out that a snowman was chasing him – and all the other policemen put on their helmets and ran out to see. They were just in time to see the frightened people rushing past – and there was the snowman galloping after them!

One policeman put out his foot as Meddle thundered past. Meddle tripped and fell over, rolling along the pavement. He was very angry.

'How dare you trip me up!' he yelled. 'I was after the robber! Now he's escaped.'

The policeman dragged Meddle into the police station. The frightened policeman, who had ran away, was most astonished to see him.

'So you weren't a snowman after all!' he said. 'You were dressed up in that white cape. Well, Mister Meddle, and what were you doing in Mister Jinks's garden, I should like to know? I suppose you weren't looking for his onions, by any chance?'

'How dare you say that,' cried Meddle. 'I was watching for the thief – and I thought you were the thief – and that's why I chased you!'

'Well, Mister Meddle, please don't go about pretending to be a snowman any more,' said the head policeman. 'You've caused enough trouble for one night, meddling like this. Anyway, Mister Jinks has locked up his shed and taken the key, so nobody can steal his onions again. You needn't bother yourself with the robber either – we caught him this evening, stealing somebody's leeks.'

'Well, really! So all my trouble was for nothing!' said Meddle indignantly. 'And I've torn my white cape and somebody's trodden on my hat – all for nothing. It's too bad.'

'It's your own fault,' said the policeman. 'You shouldn't meddle!'

'Ho!' said Meddle haughtily, and off he went home, sticking his nose high in the air. He'll never learn, will he?

Chapter 3

Mister Meddle and the Bull

Did you ever hear about Mister Meddle and the bull? It's really rather funny.

Well, one day Mister Meddle got up feeling good. 'I'd like to do a good deed today,' he thought. 'I'd like to help an old woman across the road, or carry a heavy parcel for someone, or jump into the river and save somebody from drowning. I feel good enough for all those things.'

He went out to do his shopping as usual, and he looked about for a runaway horse that he could stop. But all his horses trotted along properly and not one ran away. So that was no good.

Then he walked by the river to see if

anyone would fall in so that he could rescue them. But nobody did.

Then he looked about for anyone carrying a heavy parcel, but the only person he saw was Mr Grumps, so he pretended not to notice he was carrying anything at all.

He waited about to see if any old ladies wanted to be helped over the road, but all the old ladies he saw seemed quite able to run across by themselves. So that wasn't any good either.

Mister Meddle was most disappointed. He went home by the fields, and in the distance he saw Farmer Barley, and he thought he would ask him if he could help him at all. The farmer was in the next field but one, so Mister Meddle opened the gate of the nearest field and shut it behind him, meaning to walk across to see the farmer.

The farmer heard the click of the gate and turned to look over the hedge to see who it was.

'I say!' began Meddle shouting loudly. 'Do you want –'

But Farmer Barley didn't wait to hear what Meddle said. He yelled over the hedge: 'Mind that bull!'

Meddle looked all round, but he couldn't see any bull. The farmer shouted again.

'Didn't you hear me telling you to mind that bull?'

'Now why does he want me to mind his bull!' wondered Meddle. 'Oh – I suppose he wants to go home to his dinner or something, and would like me to mind the bull for him whilst he goes. Well, as I'm looking for something good to do, I'll do what he says.'

Meddle yelled back to Farmer Barley, 'All right. I'll mind the bull! Don't worry!'

'Right!' said the farmer, and went off down

the field towards his farm. Meddle still couldn't see any bull, though he looked hard.

But the bull had seen him! It was in a little cluster of trees, and it didn't like the look of Meddle at all!

Meddle suddenly saw the bull looking at him. He decided that it didn't look a very kind animal.

'In fact, it looks rather fierce,' thought Meddle. 'Well, I'll mind it for the farmer, but I hope it won't try to run away, or anything, because I should just hate to try and bring it back.'

The bull glared at Meddle and snorted down its nose.

'You needn't do that at me,' said Meddle to the bull. 'That's a rude noise to make at anyone minding you. Don't worry. I shan't come any nearer to you. I shall stay here and you can stay there.'

But the bull didn't think the same as Meddle! It came out of the trees with a run and snorted at Meddle again, whisking its big tail up into the air.

'I wonder if bulls are pleased when they wag their tails,' thought Meddle, feeling rather uncomfortable. 'Dogs are, I know –

but this bull doesn't look at all pleased as he wags his tail. Not a bit pleased. In fact, he looks awfully angry.'

Meddle moved away a bit. The bull moved a little nearer and gave such an alarming snort that Meddle almost jumped out of his skin.

'You're making it very difficult for me to mind you!' he shouted to the bull. 'Do behave yourself. I'm only minding you till the farmer comes back.'

The bull made up his mind that he couldn't bear Meddle in his field one minute

longer. So he snorted again and ran headlong at him, putting his head down in a horrid manner. Meddle took one look at the bull's horns and fled!

How he ran! He tore to the gate with the bull after him, and got there just as the bull did. The bull tried to help him over the gate with his horns and tore Meddle's trousers, making a big hole. Meddle tumbled to the other side of the gate with a bump. The bull put his head over the top bar and snorted all over Meddle.

'You are a disgusting and most ungrateful animal,' said Meddle angrily. 'Look what you've done to my trousers! And all because I was doing a good deed and minding you for the farmer. Well – I'm not minding you any more, so you can just do what you like! I'm going to complain about you to the farmer!'

So Meddle marched off to the farmhouse, feeling very angry indeed. He rapped on the door and the farmer opened it.

'What's the matter?' he asked.

'Plenty!' said Meddle. 'Look at my trousers – new last week, and that bull of yours chased me and tore them!'

'Well, I told you to mind him,' said the

farmer. 'You should have got out of the field before he came for you.'

'Well, I thought it would be better to mind him for you in the field,' said Meddle. 'That's what comes of trying to do you a good turn.'

'What's all this about a good turn?' said the farmer, astonished. 'I didn't want you to do me a good turn! I wanted you to get out of that field as quickly as possible before the bull turned on you. When I told you to *mind* the bull I meant you to look out that he didn't chase you!'

'Well, why didn't you say so?' said Meddle, in a rage. He turned to go and nearly fell over a fat pig.

'Mind that pig now – mind that pig!' cried the farmer.

Poor Meddle! He does get into trouble, doesn't he!

Chapter 4

Mister Meddle Has a Surprise

Mister Meddle once went to stay with his Aunt Jemima, who was very strict with him. She thought it did him good, and no doubt it did – but Meddle didn't like it at all.

His Aunt Jemima did a lot of good works. She went to read to sick people, and she took pies and soups to the poor. She knitted socks for the soldiers, and did everything she could to help other people.

When Meddle came to stay with her, she made him help her. 'You can surely do a bit of knitting,' she said. 'It's easy enough.'

But poor Meddle somehow managed to get the wool all tangled round him and lost his needles. 'Are you trying to knit yourself as well as the wool?' asked his aunt crossly, as she untangled him.

'Perhaps it would be better if I took your pies and soups out?' said Meddle, thinking that it would be much easier to carry a basket than to knit a sock.

'Well, you can't make quite such a muddle with a pie as you can with wool, I suppose,' said Aunt Jemima. 'I am making a meat pie tomorrow for poor old Mrs Cook, who is in bed with a bad leg and can't do anything for herself. You shall come with me to see her, and carry the basket for me.'

'All right, Aunt Jemima,' said Meddle, with a sigh. 'I'll come.'

So the next day Aunt Jemima made a lovely round pie, with crust on it and a pretty pattern round the edge. She took it out of the oven, and showed it to Meddle.

'I wish we could have it for dinner,' said Meddle longingly.

'Don't be greedy!' said his aunt. 'Now just put it into that basket with a lid, Meddle. It's in the cupboard over there.'

Meddle found the basket. It was oblong, and had a lid that shut down, so that whatever was inside was safe from cats or dogs. 'Put the pie in, Meddle!' called his aunt. 'And don't forget to shut the lid down. I'm going up to put on my hat. You can wait for me in the garden.'

Meddle put the pie into the basket – but he forgot to shut down the lid. He went into the garden and put the basket down for a moment whilst he unpegged his scarf from the line. He felt to see if it was dry. It was, so he knotted it round his neck.

Now, whilst he was fiddling about with his scarf, a big blackbird flew down to the basket. It put its head on one side and looked at the pie. It looked good! The blackbird stood on the pie and pecked at the crust. Beaks and tails, it was delicious!

Meddle heard his aunt coming. He remembered that she told him to be sure to shut down the lid of the basket, and he hurriedly kicked it shut with his foot. He didn't see the blackbird inside! The surprised bird found itself shut in. It went on pecking at the pie, planning to fly out as soon as the lid was opened.

'Meddle! Aren't you ready?' cried Aunt Jemima. 'Come along now. You always seem to keep me waiting.'

Meddle picked up the basket and ran down the path to join his aunt. 'Come along, come along!' she said. 'We shall miss the bus.'

'Oh, are we going to catch the bus?' said Meddle, pleased. He always liked a ride in the bus or the train. 'Oh, good!'

He trotted along beside his aunt, swinging his basket, looking out for the bus. The blackbird inside didn't at all like being swung about like that. It gave aloud cheep. Meddle was most surprised.

He looked down at the basket. But the blackbird said no more for a while, Meddle and his aunt came to the bus stop. The bus was not in sight so they both sat down on the seat.

Meddle put the basket on his knee, for he was afraid he might forget it if he put it down on the seat. The blackbird began pecking again at the crust. Peck, peck, peck!

Meddle had sharp ears. He listened to the peck-peck-peck in surprise. 'Your pie does make a funny noise,' he said to his aunt. She stared at him in surprise.

'Meddle, I do hope you're not in one of your silly moods this morning,' she said to him sharply. 'You know quite well that pies don't make a noise.'

'Cheep-cheep!' said the blackbird. Meddle looked at the basket in astonishment. His aunt was a bit deaf, so she hadn't heard anything.

'Your pie is saying "Cheep-cheep",' he told his aunt.

'That's nothing to what *you'll* be saying in a minute when I scold you hard,' said his aunt crossly. 'Telling me that pies say cheep-cheep! Hold your tongue, Meddle!'

The blackbird thought it would sing a little song. So it swelled out its black throat, opened its yellow beak and trilled out a dear little tune:

'Tirra, tirra, ju-dy, ju-dee, dooit!'

'Aunt Jemima, I do wish you'd carry this pie yourself,' said Meddle, beginning to feel alarmed. 'It's beginning to sing now!'

'*Meddle*! If you don't stop telling me ridiculous things, I'll box your big ears!' said his aunt, in a real temper. 'Pies that sing – what next?'

Luckily for Meddle, the bus came along at that moment and they got in. Meddle badly wanted to put the basket down on a seat, for he was beginning to be afraid of it now, but the bus was full, so he had to take the basket on his knee once more.

The blackbird was rather frightened by the noise of the bus, so it didn't cheep or sing for a while. But when the bus stopped, it gave a loud whistle. It was so loud that Aunt Jemima heard it. She turned to Meddle at once.

'Stop whistling! A bus is not the place to whistle in.'

'I didn't whistle,' said poor Meddle.

'Well, who did then?' said his aunt.

'The pie did,' said Meddle! His aunt glared at him. 'Meddle! Will you stop trying to be funny? First you tell me the pie cheeps – then you say it sings – and now you say it whistles! You'll be telling me it can fly next!'

Well, the blackbird took it into its head to flutter its wings and try to fly out of the basket at that moment. Meddle heard the fluttering wings in horror. Why, the pie was really doing what his aunt had said – it was flying round

and round the basket. Meddle began to tremble like a jelly, and his aunt felt him shivering against her.

'Meddle, do keep still! You are making me feel all funny, shaking like that! Whatever is the matter with you this morning?'

'It's the pie,' said poor Meddle. 'It's flying round the basket now.'

Aunt Jemima thought Meddle must be going mad. She was very glad when the bus stopped and they got out. Mrs Cook's house was quite near by. Meddle carried the basket there and thankfully put it on the table. Old Mrs Cook was in bed and she stared greedily at the basket. She felt sure that something good was in there!

'Good morning, Mrs Cook! I hope you are better!' said Aunt Jemima. 'I've brought you a pie. I can't think what's the matter with Meddle this morning, because he keeps saying that my pie cheeps, and sings, and whistles – and flies!'

The blackbird whistled loudly again. Aunt Jemima thought it was Meddle, and she scolded him. 'Now don't you dare to tell me that was the pie again!' she said. 'Open the basket and put the pie on a plate.'

But Meddle simply didn't dare to open the basket and touch that pie. He stood there, staring at his aunt, and she thought that really he must be going to be ill. So she opened the lid herself, in a rage.

And out flew the big blackbird and circled round her head! Aunt Jemima gave a scream. Mrs Cook squealed for all she was worth – and Meddle tried to run for the door and fell headlong over a stool.

He got up and looked sternly at his aunt. 'You bad woman! You cooked a blackbird in your pie! You bad woman! I suppose you remembered the twenty-four blackbirds that were baked in a pie – and you caught one and put it in! No wonder that pie sang and whistled and flew! Aunt Jemima, I'm *surprised* at you!'

And for once his aunt hadn't a single word to say. She just couldn't make it out at all.

Meddle looked into the basket and then took out the pie. The bird had pecked an enormous hole in the crust. 'Look there!' said Meddle, pointing to the hole. 'That's the hole the bird pecked so that it could get out of the pie. I think you are a most unkind person, Aunt Jemima!'

He stalked out of the house and went home – and whenever his aunt scolded him after that, Meddle would stare hard at her and say, 'Blackbirds! I haven't forgotten that, Aunt Jemima!'

And his Aunt Jemima wouldn't say a word more!

Chapter 5

Mister Meddle and the Chestnuts

Mister Meddle was very fond of roast chestnuts. He liked to make a little hole in them and put them down as close to the fire as he could without getting them burnt.

Then, when they were quite cooked through with the heat of the fire, he poked them away from the burning coal and let them cool in the fender. Then he peeled them, popped the delicious roasted nuts into his mouth and ate them.

But this year there were no chestnuts in the shops. Mister Meddle was very sad. He told his friend Jinky about it.

'You know, I'm going to miss my roast chestnuts very much,' he said. 'I just can't seem to buy any anywhere.'

'Well, don't you know any trees that grow them?' asked Mister Jinky.

'I know lots of *horse*-chestnut trees,' said Meddle. 'You know – the kind we call "conkers" when they fall to the ground and split open their prickly cases – but I don't know any trees that grow eating chestnuts. Do you?'

'Oh, yes,' said Jinky. 'I'll tell you. You know the Bluebell Wood, don't you?'

'Yes,' said Meddle.

'Well, go right through it till you come to the big oak tree in the middle,' said Jinky. 'Then turn to the right, go down the little path there, and you'll soon come to two or three big eating-chestnut trees.'

'How shall I know them?' asked Meddle. 'They are not like horse-chestnuts, are they?'

'Not a bit,' said Jinky. 'You'll know them, my dear Meddle, because they are growing the eating chestnuts you love!'

'Are they in prickly cases like the conkers?' said Meddle.

'They are in cases, but much, much more

prickly ones than the conkers,' said Jinky. 'What a lot of questions you ask, Meddle.'

'Well, I want to be sure I don't make a mistake,' said Meddle. 'I'm always making mistakes – and I'm trying not to now.'

Well, that afternoon Meddle took his biggest basket and set off to Bluebell Wood. He took the little path to the right when he came to the oak tree, and very soon he arrived at the three chestnut trees. Their

leaves were quite different from the conker trees he knew – but Meddle couldn't help knowing they were the right trees, because under them were scattered heaps and heaps of eating chestnuts, some still in their prickly brown cases, and others tumbled out, dark brown and shiny.

'My word, I shall have a lovely lot to take home and roast!' said Meddle, pleased. He began to gather them up and put them into his basket.

'What nice big ones there are!' thought Meddle. 'And oh, my goodness me, look at *that* one!'

Now the one that Meddle was looking at wasn't a chestnut in a case at all. It was a small, brown, prickly hedgehog that had wandered up. As soon as it saw Meddle it had curled itself up tightly, so that it was nothing but a round ball of prickles. There it lay on the ground, perfectly still, looking for all the world like a very big chestnut case, all prickly.

Meddle picked it up. The prickles hurt his fingers, so he soon dropped it into the basket. 'What a giant chestnut must be inside this prickly case!' he thought. 'I'll open it when I get home, and see what kind of a chestnut

43

there is there. Maybe there are two or three. What a find!'

He carried his basket home. The hedgehog didn't move at all. It was frightened. It knew that as long as it stayed tightly curled up, nobody could harm it. So there it lay in the basket, looking just like a big prickly chestnut.

When Meddle got home he was hungry. 'I really think I will roast a few chestnuts at once,' he said. 'I feel as if I could eat a whole lot. I'll open this great big one first and see how many nuts there are inside it.'

But, of course, he couldn't open it! The more he tried, the more tightly the hedgehog curled itself up. And Meddle pricked his fingers so badly that they began to bleed.

'You horrid chestnut!' said Meddle, crossly. 'I'll just put you straight down beside the fire as you are – and you'll have to open then, and I'll get your nuts!'

So down beside the fire went the hedgehog, along with a handful of nuts. Meddle sat down to watch them roast.

Now the hedgehog didn't like the fire at all. It was much too hot. It lay and thought what would be the best thing to do. It didn't want to be cooked. It didn't want to open itself and be caught. But as the fire felt hotter and hotter, the poor hedgehog knew there was only one thing to do – and at once!

'I must crawl away, I really must!' it thought. So it opened out a little, put out its funny little snout, and began to crawl away from the hearth.

Meddle suddenly saw it. He thought he must be dreaming. He rubbed his eyes and looked again. The hedgehog was still crawling.

'My chestnut's walking!' yelled Meddle. Then he saw the little creature's nose, and he gave a yell.

'My chestnut's got a nose! It's got eyes! Goodness, gracious, it's grown legs, too!'

The hedgehog tried to get over the hearthrug. Meddle gave another yell and rushed out of the house. He bumped into Jinky, and held on to him tight.

'*Now* what's the matter?' said Jinky in surprise.

'My big chestnut is walking on the hearthrug!' cried Meddle.

'Don't be silly,' said Jinky.

'And it's got a nose,' said Meddle, clinging

to Jinky, for he really felt very frightened.

'You must be mad,' said Jinky. 'Whoever heard of a chestnut with a nose?'

'And it's got eyes and legs too,' said poor Meddle. 'Oh, Jinky, it must be magic. Oh, I don't like it.'

'I'll come and see this peculiar chestnut,' said Jinky. So he went into Meddle's house and looked around. But the hedgehog had heard him coming and had curled itself up tightly under a chair.

Jinky looked at it. 'There is is!' said Meddle,

pointing. 'But how funny – it hasn't got eyes, or a nose or legs, any more.'

Jinky knew at once that it was a hedgehog. How he grinned to himself! 'We'll soon make it grow eyes and nose and legs again,' he said. 'Get me a saucer of bread and milk for your giant chestnut, Meddle.'

'Bread and milk for a chestnut to eat!' said Meddle, in the greatest surprise. 'Whatever are you talking about?'

'Go and get it,' said Jinky. So Meddle went to his larder and soon came back with a saucer of bread and milk. Jinky set it down beside the tightly curled hedgehog. The hedgehog smelt the food. It uncurled itself. Out came a little nose.

Meddle gave a squeal. 'Look! It's come alive again!'

The hedgehog went to the saucer on its short little legs and began to eat the bread and milk. Meddle watched in the greatest surprise, his eyes nearly falling out of his head.

When the hedgehog had finished the bread and milk, Jinky took out his handkerchief. He wrapped it round the little prickly creature, and lifted it up. The prickles were caught in the handkerchief and did not hurt him.

'If you don't want this giant chestnut, I'll have it,' he said.

'Take it with pleasure!' cried Meddle. 'I don't want such a peculiar thing in my house. You seem to know what to do with it, anyway.'

'Well, I've always liked hedgehogs,' said Jinky with a grin. 'They eat all the slugs and grubs in the garden! I never heard of anybody but gipsies trying to roast a hedgehog before! Another of your little mistakes, I'm afraid, Meddle!'

And off he went, grinning so broadly that his smile reached each of his ears. Well, well, well – what will old Meddle do next? I simply can't imagine, can you?

Chapter 6

Mister Meddle and the Kangaroo

Once upon a time there was a travelling circus that passed near to the town where Mister Meddle lived. Mister Meddle didn't know anything about it, because the circus didn't stop.

But, as it went by the town, the performing kangaroo escaped from its cage! Nobody saw it go. It found that its door hadn't been locked, so it just pushed it open and went out. It hopped right over the nearby hedge with one bound and then jumped in glee over three fields and a stream.

Now, Mister Meddle was just out for his morning walk. He was trying to make up a poem that went like this:

'The wind was soft and warm,
The sky was very blue,
The birds were singing sweet . . .'

Mister Meddle got as far as those three lines and there he stuck. He just simply could *not* think of a fourth line.

He began again

'The wind was soft and warm,
The sky was very blue,
The birds were singing sweet –
IS THAT A KANGAROO?'

Now Mister Meddle didn't mean the last line to rhyme like that, and it really sounded very funny. But he didn't think about its being funny – all he thought about was the very peculiar sight in front of him. Jumping down the field path was a large kangaroo!

Mister Meddle was not used to meeting kangaroos in the fields. He stood still and stared at it.

'Now, I must think about this,' said Mister Meddle. 'Kangaroos don't live in this country. Therefore that can't be a kangaroo. On the other hand, it's not a rabbit or a hedgehog. And it does really look extremely like a kangaroo.'

The kangaroo bounded nearer. It jumped right over a hedge and back again. Meddle began to feel a little scared. He didn't know how to treat kangaroos. Did you pat them like a dog? Or stroke them like a cat? Or prod them like a pig?

'Now I really *must* think about this,' said Meddle firmly. 'That *is* a kangaroo, but it can't be a real one. So I must be dreaming.

Of course – that's what it is! I'm asleep and dreaming. It's only a dream kangaroo. Well, I'm not frightened of a dream kangaroo. Not a bit! Ho – I've only got to wake up and it will be gone.'

The kangaroo bounded almost on top of Meddle, and stared at him in rather a fierce manner. Meddle stared back.

'Stare all you like!' he said to the kangaroo. 'But let me tell you this – you're not real! Not a bit real. You're only a dream.' My dream! Ha ha, ho ho!'

The kangaroo put its face near to Meddle's and made a horrid sort of noise. Meddle jumped back a little.

'If you do that sort of thing to me I'll wake up and then you'll be gone like a puff of smoke!' he said. 'Do you want to be gone? Just be careful, please. I don't like you very much, and I may wake up with a jump. Then you'll be gone for ever.'

'Grr-rrr-rrr-rrr!' said the kangaroo, and put up its fists as if it were going to fight Meddle. It was a very clever kangaroo, and could box with its fists just like a man. It often boxed with its keeper, and it really thought that Meddle would enjoy boxing too.

But Meddle didn't like boxing at all. He stepped back a bit further. The kangaroo followed.

'*Will* you keep away from me?' roared Meddle, getting angry. 'You're a most annoying dream. I'll slap you if you keep following me. Now, I'm going to turn my back on you, and walk away. Maybe when I turn round you'll have changed into a pig or a cat or something, like things always do in dreams. So just look out!'

Meddle turned his back and walked away, hoping and hoping that the kangaroo would turn into a harmless mouse. But no sooner had he walked two steps than he felt a tremendous punch on his right shoulder. He nearly fell over.

He turned round in a rage. The kangaroo was dancing about all round him, aiming at him with its fists, enjoying itself very much. Meddle shouted at it.

'What do you want to punch me like that for? You might have woken me up! You know I'm asleep and dreaming, don't you? I wish I could wake up. You're a very horrid dream.'

The kangaroo gave him another punch, right in his middle this time. Meddle bent

over with a groan. 'You horrid creature! You don't know how to play fair, even! Take that – and that.'

Meddle hit out at the kangaroo, who was simply delighted. He gave Meddle such a punch that the poor man went right through the hedge and out at the other side! Two men were coming over the field there and they stared in great surprise at Meddle flying through the hedge.

'Do you usually come through hedges like that?' asked one of the men, at last.

'Of course not,' said Meddle. 'I'm having a very nasty dream, that's all. I can't imagine why you've come into my dream too. Really, I do wish I *could* wake up! I've already dreamt a kangaroo, and he keeps punching me.'

'Dreamt a kangaroo!' cried one of the men. 'Why, we are looking for a kangaroo! Where is he?'

'Oh, for goodness' sake don't call him!' said Meddle. 'He's gone out of my dream for a moment and I really don't want him back.'

'You must be mad,' said one of the men. 'You're not dreaming! You're wide awake.'

'Now look here – I met a kangaroo just now, and I should never do that if I was awake,' said Meddle. 'I tell you, I'm dreaming. Pinch me, please. You can't feel pinches in dreams. Pinch me hard. I shan't feel it, and then you'll know I'm in a dream.'

The men pinched Meddle as hard as they could. He gave a loud yell. 'Ow! Don't! You're hurting me!'

'Well, there you are!' said the men. 'You're not dreaming! Now – where's our kangaroo? He's escaped from our travelling circus.'

Meddle stared at the men with his mouth wide open in surprise and horror. 'Do you mean to say that was a real live kangaroo I saw?' he said at last. 'I didn't dream him? Good gracious, I hit him! He might have eaten me up!'

The men laughed. 'He wouldn't have done that,' they said. 'But you were mighty brave to hit him. He's very strong, and can be quite fierce. Look – here he comes, over the hedge!'

Sure enough, there was the kangaroo, leaping high over the hedge. He jumped to the men, and put his big arms round the one who was his keeper.

'Shake hands with this gentleman,' the keeper said to the kangaroo. But Meddle wasn't going to have any more to do with kangaroos at all! He fled through the hedge again and tore home as fast as he could.

But you should have heard him boasting the next day!

'I was walking along making up a poem,' he told his friends. 'This was the poem:

'The wind was soft and warm,
The sky was very blue,
The birds were singing sweet . . .
IS THAT A KANGAROO?'

'But why did you put a kangaroo suddenly into your poem?' asked his friends.

'Because there *was* one, an escaped one!' said Meddle.' Ah, you should have seen me! I went up to him. I ordered him to come with me, and when he wouldn't, I fought him. Slap, bang. I hit him hard. When his keepers came, I handed over the kangaroo to them at once. I shouldn't be surprised if they asked me to join their circus.'

But Meddle didn't tell anyone at all that he had thought the kangaroo was a dream. Wasn't he funny?

Chapter 7

Mister Meddle Makes Another Mistake

Once Mister Meddle felt rather gloomy, and he went about with such a long face that his friends teased him about it.

'Whatever is the matter?' they asked. 'Have you lost a pound and found fifty pence?'

'Don't be silly,' said Mister Meddle. 'I am sad because I am bored.'

'Look here, Meddle,' said Gobo at once, 'you haven't enough to do! That's what's the matter with *you*! You get a job of some kind – or go round helping people. That's the best cure for being bored or sad.'

'Is it really?' said Mister Meddle. 'Well, I'll do that then. I see that Biscuit, the grocer, wants another errand boy. Perhaps I could take that job.'

So off he went to Mr Biscuit, and the grocer said yes, he could be an errand boy.

'What have I to do?' asked Meddle, quite excited.

'Nothing much, except to take parcels round,' said Biscuit. 'This is Sam Quickly, my other errand boy. He's a good lad. You can help him today for a start.'

Well, as you know, Meddle was a muddler – and as Sam Quickly was just like his name, the two didn't get on very well together.

Sam did everything smartly and quickly – but old Meddle fell over sacks, trod on spilt potatoes instead of picking them up, and covered himself with flour almost at once.

'Good gracious! You look like a miller!' said Sam with a giggle. 'Here, take this parcel to Mrs Brown's, and for goodness' sake dust yourself before you go!'

Meddle dusted himself so hard that the flour flew all over the place and Sam sneezed. Then Meddle took the parcel and went off to Mrs Brown's.

But it was a very long way and before long

Meddle began to puff and pant. When a bus came along he hopped into it.

'I shall wear out all my shoes if I walk so far,' said Meddle, sitting down with a sigh. 'How tired my feet are already!'

The bus was full. An old lady got in and glared at Meddle because he had put his parcel down beside him, so that there was hardly any room for her.

'Move that parcel!' she said sharply.

'Sorry,' said Meddle, and he picked up the parcel. He decided to sit on it, then there would be plenty of room. So he sat down on it. It made rather a peculiar noise, but that didn't worry Meddle. No, he just sat there happily.

Then he began to feel rather wet. He looked down at the seat and to his horror he found something bright yellow was dripping off the seat to the floor! The yolk of eggs! Good gracious – surely there weren't eggs in that parcel!

He got up in a hurry – and the parcel stuck to him! Meddle undid the paper quickly – and there, in the parcel, was a bag of twelve broken eggs, a bag of flour soaked with the eggs, a split bag of sugar, and half a pound of butter! The butter looked very strange indeed, for Meddle was quite heavy.

'Bother!' said Meddle. He picked up the spoilt parcel and got off the bus. He ran all the way back to Mr Biscuit's and showed him the parcel.

'How was I to know there were eggs in it?' he said. 'They have spoilt my trousers!'

'Serves you right,' said Mr Biscuit angrily.

'What do I care about your trousers! Nothing at all! What I *do* care about is that you have spoilt Mrs Brown's goods. Sam! Sam! Make up another parcel for Mrs Brown and take it yourself. This poor, silly creature thinks parcels are to be sat on, not delivered.'

Mister Meddle was angry. How dare Mr Biscuit talk about him like that! He made up his mind to show him what he could do when he tried. Poor, silly creature indeed!

'Make up two ounces of pepper for Mrs Jones,' said the grocer to Meddle. 'And look sharp about it! It's in that drawer there.'

Meddle went to the big drawer where the pepper was kept. It was lined with tin, and there was a scoop inside for measuring out the pepper.

Just as Meddle was taking up the scoop to measure the pepper, a large bluebottle came buzzing around. Now, Meddle simply hated bluebottles. He hated their buzz, and he hated their great fat bodies.

'I'll pepper you if you come near me!' said Meddle fiercely. 'Keep away!'

The bluebottle at once flew round Meddle's head. 'Zz-zz-zz-zz!' it said boldly. 'Zz-zz-zz-zz!'

'All right!' said Meddle, in a rage. 'I'll pepper you then!'

He threw a scoopful of pepper at the bluebottle. It flew off and came back again. 'Zz-zz-zz-zz! Zz-zz-zz-zz!'

'Get away, I tell you, get away!' yelled Meddle. He threw another lot of pepper at the bluebottle – and most unfortunately he didn't see Mr Biscuit coming by, and the poor grocer found pepper flying all round him. He glared at Meddle and began to shout at him – and then he sneezed, and sneezed, and sneezed!

'You bad fellow –' he began, 'you – a-tishoo! A-tish-oo! You bad – a-tishoo! Wait till I get you. A-tishoo!' Some customers came in and they began to sneeze too. How they sneezed! They sneezed so much that they had to go out of the shop without buying anything, and that made Mr Biscuit crosser than ever. He gave the surprised Meddle a good scolding.

'Stop playing about with the pepper!' he cried. 'Go out and ask Sam to give you another job in the yard!'

So out went Meddle, sneezing hard himself. Sam was already back from Mrs

Brown's, and he looked in surprise at the sneezing Meddle.

'Got a cold?' he asked. 'Good gracious, what a sneeze you've got – sounds like fireworks going off! Now come along and do some work. All these sacks of goods have got to be taken to the storehouse down the road, where Mr Biscuit keeps a good many things.

Meddle looked at the sacks. Well, that seemed easy enough. He could carry a sack as well as anyone. Here goes! Up went a sack on his shoulder, and Meddle staggered off down the yard, out of the gate, and off to the shed down the road.

The sack was full of potatoes. It was very heavy. Meddle was glad to put it down when he reached the shed. He made up his mind that he wouldn't choose potatoes again – no, not he! He would choose a bag of sago or something that was much lighter.

Sam didn't seem to feel the weight of the sacks at all. He was a good and cheerful worker and he went up and down with the sacks, whistling merrily.

Meddle went round the sacks to feel which ones were the lightest of all. He chose a light one and went off with it. That was better! The next time he again chose a light sack, so that Sam had to take all the heavy ones.

'Look here,' said Sam at last, 'I'm carrying all the heavy ones and you're picking the light ones. That won't do!'

'All right. I'll take a heavy one this time,' said Meddle, and he picked up a sack that he knew was very, very light indeed. It was full of new sponges, dry and light as feathers! But Meddle pretended that it was very heavy

indeed, and groaned as he lifted the sack to his shoulder.

Sam knew the sack was full of dry sponges. He knew it wasn't heavy – Meddle was just pretending. Sam was about to shout at Meddle when something fell on his head – a big drop of rain. Then Sam grinned and said nothing at all. It was going to rain, was it? Well, let Meddle take the sponges then, and see what happened! He'd be rather surprised!

Meddle went off with the sack of sponges, smiling. Aha! He had the lightest sack of all, as light as a feather! It wouldn't take him long to run down the street with *that*!

It began to rain heavily. Thunder crashed overhead and the rain became so heavy that a little rivulet trickled down Meddle's nose and ran off the end.

Now you know what happens to your sponge when you fill it with water – it gets very heavy and very wet! Meddle had a whole *sackful* of sponges – and they began to get very wet indeed!

The wetter they got with the rain, the heavier they felt. Meddle was carrying a whole rainstorm in those sponges! He staggered along with the sack, which got heavier and heavier every minute. Meddle couldn't understand it!

'Now how can a sack change from light to heavy without my putting anything into it?' he said to himself. 'I can't understand it!'

The rain fell more heavily, and the sponges in the sack soaked up the pelting drops and almost dragged Meddle down to the ground. He staggered along, his knees bending under him. Behind him came Sam Quickly, squealing with laughter, for he knew exactly what was happening.

At last the sponges were so heavy and so big with rain that the sack could no longer hold them. It burst – and Meddle was buried under a pile of great wet sponges! When the wet, cold, slithery things slid over him, Meddle gave a yell.

'What is it – what is it? What have I been carrying? Frogs? Toads? Fish? Oh, they've come alive and they are out of the sack! Help, help!'

Meddle scrambled up and rushed home in great fright. Sam Quickly laughed so much that he had to put his own sack down and wipe his eyes. Then he squeezed out the sponges and fetched a fresh sack for them.

'That's the last we'll see of our new errand boy!' said Sam to himself. 'And a good thing too!'

He was right. Meddle didn't go near Mr Biscuit's again. He sat by the fire to dry his things and looked gloomily into the flames.

'Well, work's all right for some people,' said Meddle to himself, 'but it's no good for me. I've got too many brains to be an errand boy!'

It's a great pity that Mr Biscuit doesn't sell brains – if he did, Sam Quickly would buy some and deliver them at Meddle's house, I'm sure!

Chapter 8

Mister Meddle's Umbrella

When Mister Meddle went to stay with his Aunt Jemima, she was very strict with him. She made him put on galoshes when it was wet, and a hat when it was sunny, and a scarf round his throat when the wind was cold.

'I wish you wouldn't fuss!' Meddle kept saying. 'Aunt Jemima, I wish you wouldn't FUSS!'

'Meddle, you are so silly that I'm sure I don't know what would happen to you if I didn't fuss,' said his aunt. 'I am *not* going to have you in bed with colds while you are staying here – so I am going to fuss all I like, and you will have to do as you are told.'

Now if there was one thing more than

anything that Meddle hated, it was taking an
umbrella out with him. He simply couldn't
bear it.

'If I have to carry an umbrella it's a perfect
nuisance!' he said. 'It gets between my ankles
and trips me up. It digs itself into people as I
pass them, and they get angry with me. I just
can't bear an umbrella.'

'Well, my dear Meddle, you'll have to take
one this afternoon when you go out, because
it's simply pouring with rain!' said his aunt
firmly. 'Look at it – pouring cats and dogs.'

'I wish it really *would* pour cats and dogs,'

said Meddle. 'I've always wanted to see that, and I never have. I shan't go out this afternoon, Aunt Jemima, if you make me take an umbrella.'

'Very well,' said his aunt. 'Then you can't call at the book shop and get your *Sunny Stories.*'

'Oh, I simply *must* have that,' said Meddle. 'Why, I might be in the book this week.'

Well, it was still raining that afternoon when Meddle put his coat on, and told Aunt Jemima he was going out. His aunt went to the hall stand and fetched her umbrella. It was a fat red one, and had a bright red, crooked handle. She gave it to him.

'You'll get wet through if you don't take this,' she said. 'Go along now. Hurry up!'

'Bother!' said Meddle. 'Bother, bother, bother. I do so hate umbrellas.'

'Meddle, if you don't take it, you don't go out!' said Aunt Jemima. So Meddle took it, and went down the garden path. He began thinking about a story he was going to write. It was to be about a soldier who was very brave.

'He shall have a sword,' said Meddle to himself. 'An enormous sword. And he will use it like this – slash, slash, poke, poke, slash, slash!'

Meddle began to slash about with the umbrella as if it were a sword. My, he did feel grand. People stared at him in surprise as they passed, but Meddle didn't even see them.

'My soldier shall fight well!' he cried. 'Slash, slash!'

He nearly knocked old Mrs Jinks's hat off her head, and she scurried away in fright. Meddle went all the way to the bookshop in the pouring rain, pretending that the umbrella was a sword. He didn't even put it up. He soon was quite soaked, and the rain dripped down his neck.

So, of course, when he got home again, his coat was dripping and his hair was so wet that it looked dreadful.

'Meddle! Didn't you put up your umbrella?' cried his aunt angrily. 'Oh, you silly creature! What's the use of taking out an umbrella if you don't put it up? Now you will get a dreadful cold.'

'A-tish-oo!' said Meddle, with a sneeze. And the next day he was in bed, feeling very bad.

Well, when he was up, and wanted to go out

for a walk, his Aunt Jemima looked up at the sky. 'Meddle,' she said, 'it looks like rain. I don't think I can trust you to go out. You'll only get wet again.'

'Aunt Jemima, if only you'll let me go out and buy a bag of boiled sweets, I promise I'll take an umbrella,' said Meddle.

'But will you put it up?' asked his aunt. 'You took an umbrella last time, but you didn't put it up. And what's the use of that? Last time you said your umbrella was a sword. This time you may pretend it's a lamp post or something.'

Well, Meddle got his way. He took the fat red umbrella out of the hall stand and went off. It wasn't raining, but after a little some drops began to fall. Meddle was busy putting his hand into the bag to get out a nice red sweet, and he was cross.

'Stupid rain!' he said. 'Well, I promised my aunt to put up the umbrella, so I must.'

Meddle held up his umbrella above his head, but he didn't put it up! He just held it up like a stick, without opening the umbrella at all. He was so busy with his sweets that he forgot that an umbrella must be opened when it is held up. So there he was, going down the road, getting wetter and wetter, his umbrella held unopened above his head.

'Well, well,' said Meddle to himself. 'What's the use of an umbrella, after all, I'd like to know? I'm getting just as wet as if I'd not taken one with me at all. Splash, splash, splash, the rain comes down – and I'm getting soaked.'

Now Aunt Jemima was watching for Meddle when he came home – and when she saw him walking up the path with his umbrella held

like a stick over his head, she was really very angry. Meddle saw her frowning and he was puzzled.

'Now what's the matter, Aunt?' he cried, as he walked up the path and saw her looking out of the window. 'I took the umbrella, didn't I? And I put it up, didn't I? But what's the use – I'm just as wet as ever!'

'My dear Meddle, you might as well take a toothpick to hold over your head as an umbrella, if you don't bother to put it up,' said his aunt. 'Look up and see your umbrella.'

So Meddle looked up, and saw that he had forgotten to open the umbrella, and he felt rather foolish. 'Dear me,' he said. 'I've been rather silly.'

'You'll have a cold tomorrow,' said Aunt Jemima.

'A-tish-oo!' said Meddle. And, of course, he was in bed with a cold the very next day.

Well, well. Aunt Jemima was very cross and not a bit nice to Meddle. When he was up again, she spoke to him very sternly.

'Meddle, every time you go out in future you will take an umbrella with you,' she said. 'And you will practise putting it up and down, up and down, before you go out. Then perhaps you will remember that an umbrella is meant to be opened when it is in use.'

So Meddle practised putting the umbrella up and down, and opened and shut it a dozen times before he went out. The cat hated it. It was a great shock to her whenever Meddle suddenly opened the umbrella just in front of her.

When Meddle's cold was better enough for him to go out, his aunt made him take the umbrella with him.

'But it isn't raining!' said Meddle. 'No, Aunt, I'd look silly.'

'You'll look a lot sillier if you get a third cold, and miss your birthday party,' said Aunt Jemima. 'Take the umbrella, and don't make a fuss, Meddle.

So Meddle took it with him, though the sun was shining brightly. He went to visit his friend Gobo, and he sat and talked to him for a long time. And, of course, when he left to go home, he quite forgot to take the umbrella with him. He left it behind in Gobo's hall-stand!

And when he was almost home the rain came down. How it poured! You should have seen it. Meddle got quite a shock when he felt the big raindrops stinging his face.

'Ha! Good thing I took an umbrella with me!' he said. 'A very good thing indeed. I'll put it up.'

But the umbrella wasn't there to put up. Meddle stared all round as if he thought the umbrella would come walking up. But of course it didn't.

'Bother!' said Meddle. 'Where's it gone? I know I had it when I left home. How can I put an umbrella up if it isn't here? My goodness! What will Aunt Jemima say when she sees me coming home in the rain without the umbrella? I wonder if she's looking out of the window. I won't peep and see in case she is. I'll run all the way back to Gobo's and see if I've left the umbrella there!'

If only Meddle had looked he would have seen his aunt knocking at the window to tell him to run quickly up the garden path and come in out of the rain! Instead of that, he ran down the road again, and went all the way back to Gobo's with the rain pouring down on him. How wet he got! He dripped like a piece of seaweed.

By the time he got to Gobo's he was wet

through and shivering. He banged at the door. Gobo opened it.

'I've come back for my umbrella before I get wet,' said Meddle.

'You silly! You're soaked already,' said Gobo. 'As for your umbrella, I've sent Mrs Gobo to your aunt's with it. You must have missed her. I can't lend you one because I haven't one at the moment. My goodness, won't you get wet!'

So Meddle had to run back in the rain without an umbrella at all, and his shoes went squelch, squelch, squelch, and his coat went drip, drip, drip.

How angry his Aunt Jemima was when he came in. 'Meddle! I send you out with an umbrella, and you come home in the pouring rain without it, and I knock at the window to tell you to come in, and you run off down the road again, and then Mrs Gobo comes in with your umbrella, and you come home again as wet as a sponge. You'll get a very bad cold.'

'A-tish-oo!' said Meddle at once. 'A-tish-oo! I must go and get a hanky!'

And, of course, he was in bed with a bad cold the next day and missed his birthday party after all! Now he is packing up to go home because his aunt says she won't keep him any longer. Do you know what she gave him for a birthday present? Guess! An umbrella – and the handle is a donkey's head.

'I chose a donkey because I really thought it would suit you well,' said Aunt Jemima.

But I expect he will leave it in the bus, don't you?

Chapter 9

Mister Meddle Does a Bit of Good

Once there came a magician to Meddle's village. He was very clever, and knew a great deal of magic. His name was Sneaky, and he was just like his name.

He was not a nice person. He was mean to everybody, and they couldn't be mean back, because they were afraid of him. They stayed in their houses when Sneaky came by, because they were so afraid he might take them to be his servants.

But, of course Meddle didn't stay in *his* house. Oh no! – he was far too curious about Sneaky. He longed to see what he was like. So when he knew that the magician was coming down the road, Meddle hopped out of his front door and squeezed himself inside a bush, so that he might peep out at Sneaky.

Sneaky wore very soft shoes that made no sound. Meddle couldn't hear him coming at all. 'I must peep out and see if he has gone by,' said Meddle at last. So he poked out his head – and just at that very moment Sneaky came by! He saw Meddle peeping out of the bush and he stopped and grinned.

'Ho! Spying on me! This won't do, my dear fellow, this won't do!'

'I'm s-s-s-s-orry!' said Meddle, shivering in his shoes. 'I j-j-j-just wanted to s-s-s-see what you were l-l-l-like!'

'Oh, you wanted to see what I was like, did you?' said Sneaky. 'Well, you just come home with me, and you'll soon see what I am like! I need a servant.'

And to Meddle's dismay Sneaky reached out a long arm, picked him out of the bush, tucked him under his arm like a parcel and went off with him.

'Well, it serves Meddle right,' said everyone, peeping from their windows. 'He is always prying and meddling!'

Poor Meddle! He didn't like being the

magician's servant at all. He wasn't very good at cooking. He wasn't very good at cleaning. He didn't remember anything he was told, and he was always poking his nose into the magician's books and spells.

'One day you'll leave your nose behind you, if you poke it into any more of my magic,' said Sneaky angrily, when he found Meddle reading one of his magic books. 'Go about your work. Clean my broomsticks today, and all the furniture too. It looks dreadful! Look at those smears! Look at those stains!'

'Y-y-y-yes, sir,' said Meddle. 'B-b-but I haven't any more p-p-p-polish.'

'What a nuisance you are!' said Sneaky. 'Always wanting some more of this, and some more of that. I will give you some polish today – and you must make it last for a whole week.'

Sneaky went to a cupboard. He took out two tins. One was blue and one was green.

'Now listen carefully,' he said sternly to Meddle. 'This blue tin is for my broomsticks. It is a fly-away polish, and has magic in it, so that when I want to use my broomsticks to fly away on, they will go smoothly and swiftly through the air. And this polish, in the green

tin, is a good, bright polish for the furniture.
Now go away and work hard.'

'Yes, sir,' said Meddle, and he took the tins
of polish. He went to the kitchen. He sighed
deeply. He hated polishing. He looked at the
clock – four o'clock, tea-time!

'I really must have a cup of tea first,' said
Meddle. Just then he heard the front door
bang, and he ran to the window. 'Ha! There's
old Sneaky going out! Good! Now I can have
a cup of tea in peace.

He made himself a pot of tea. He sat back
on a chair, put his feet on a stool, and took up

his cup. Ah, this was nice – almost like being at home!

But just then he heard the sound of a key being slid into a lock – Sneaky was back again already! Meddle leapt up in a great hurry, spilt the tea all down himself, and rushed to get his polishing cloths. If Sneaky found him lazing instead of polishing, how angry he would be!

Meddle opened the two tins of polish. He stole quietly into the dining-room, where Sneaky kept his magic broomsticks. Then he looked at the tins of polish.

'Goodness!' said Meddle, scratching his head. 'Now which was which? Was the blue tin the fly-away polish, or the green?'

He simply *couldn't* remember. He didn't dare to go and ask. He stood there and stared at both tins.

'Well, *I* think Sneaky said the green polish was for his broomsticks, and the blue polish was for the furniture,' said Meddle at last. 'I'll do the broomsticks first.'

He began to polish the broomsticks with the green polish. They shone and glittered. Meddle did all six of the broomsticks, and then turned to the furniture. He dabbed his cloth into the tin of blue polish. It was the fly-away polish, of course, but Meddle didn't think it was.

'I'll polish Sneaky's oak chair first,' said Meddle to himself. 'That's about the most important piece of furniture in the room.'

So he began to polish the big armchair with the blue polish. My word, how that chair shone and gleamed! It was marvellous polish. And it was magic too – for whoever sat down in that chair would now fly away in it, goodness knew where.

'Oooh, I'm tired,' said Meddle at last. 'My arm aches. I must have a little rest. I'll pretend to be Sneaky and sit down in his chair. How important I shall feel!'

Meddle was just about to sit down in Sneaky's chair, when the magician himself came into the room. How he glared at Meddle!

'What! You are daring to sit in my chair!' he cried. 'Get out at once!'

He pushed Meddle so hard that the poor fellow went spinning into a corner, and fell over all the broomsticks there. They tumbled across him with a clatter.

'Ha ha!' laughed Sneaky, sitting down hard

in his char. 'How funny you look, Meddle!'

But his laughter soon stopped, and a frightened look came on his face. His chair was rising into the air! 'Hi! What's this? Stop, stop!' yelled Sneaky. But the chair didn't stop. It flew up to the ceiling. Bang! It made a hole there! It flew through the hole, up, up, to the roof!

'You wicked meddler, you've polished my chair with the fly-away polish!' yelled Sneaky in a rage. 'Wait till I jump out and catch you!'

But it was too late for him to jump out.

Crash! The chair flew through the roof, and a shower of tiles fell down. Meddle stared in the greatest surprise. He ran to the door and looked upwards. There was Sneaky flying away in the old oak chair – up, up, up to the clouds! He got smaller and smaller, the further he went.

'Ooooh,' said Meddle, hardly believing his eyes. He sat down on the grass and wiped his forehead. 'Ooooooh. He's gone. Simply gone. Just like that! And all because I used the wrong polish. Well, well, well! It seems as if it's a good thing to be silly sometimes!'

The folk in Meddle's village saw the curious sight of Sneaky flying through the roof of his house, away up to the sky. They came running to Sneaky's house, and there they saw Meddle sitting on the grass.

'What's happened? What's happened?' they cried.

'Well, you see, I polished Sneaky's chair with the wrong polish,' explained Meddle. 'I used the fly-away polish instead of the furniture polish. I am always so foolish.'

'Why, Meddle, that was the cleverest thing you've ever done!' cried everyone.

'But I didn't mean to be clever,' said

Meddle honestly. 'It was a mistake!'

'Good old Meddle, fine old Meddle!' cried everyone, and they all crowded round him and shook hands.

'Come to tea with me tomorrow,' said one.

'Come and have some of my ripe plums,' said another.

'Come and have a cup of cocoa with me,' said a third.

Meddle was most astonished. He wasn't used to being made a fuss of. He liked it. It was nice.

'Thank you, kind friends,' he said. 'I think that now I've done *one* clever thing, I may perhaps be cleverer in the future. Anyway, I'll try!'

So he's trying, and not getting on so badly either. I'll be sure and tell you if he starts meddling and getting into trouble again.

Chapter 10

You're a Nuisance, Mister Meddle

Once Mister Meddle was going down the lane, past Farmer Corny's apple orchard, when he saw a spire of smoke rising up from the village not far off.

'My!' said Mister Meddle to himself, 'that looks as if someone's house is on fire!'

Three small boys came up, and Mister Meddle spoke to them. 'Have you come from the village? Is anyone's house on fire?'

'Don't know,' said the biggest boy. He turned to look at the spire of smoke. Then he looked at Meddle. Then he looked into the apple orchard, where apples hung ripe and red. He saw there a ladder going up a tree, and at the top of it was Farmer Corny himself, picking apples.

Then the little boy spoke again to Meddle. 'Well, maybe there *is* a house on fire!' he said. 'Maybe there is someone that wants rescuing! Maybe they haven't a ladder to rescue them with! Whatever will they do?'

Meddle thought it would be fine to be a hero and rescue someone from a burning house. He could see himself going up a long ladder, jumping into a smoky window and

coming out with someone over his shoulder. How the crowd would cheer him! How important he would feel!'

'I wish I had a ladder,' said Meddle. 'You can't rescue people from burning houses without a ladder –'

'Look, mister, there's a ladder!' said the naughty little boy, and he pointed to the one in the orchard nearby. 'You could take that one!'

'So I could, so I could!' said Meddle. 'What a sharp little boy you are!'

Meddle jumped over the wall and ran to the ladder. He didn't see the farmer up the tree. He pulled away the ladder and put it over his shoulder.

The farmer saw someone walking off with his ladder and yelled out angrily.

'Hi! Bring that back at once! What do you mean by going off with my ladder?'

'Just going to rescue someone from a burning house!' yelled back Meddle. 'I'll bring it back soon. You go on picking your apples!'

The farmer was very angry, but he couldn't get down from the tree because the branches were so high above the ground. The little boys gave Meddle a cheer as he went over the wall with the ladder and set off down the lane. He felt quite a hero already.

The naughty little boys saw the farmer was safely up a high tree and couldn't get down. So up into the smaller trees they went and were soon stuffing their pockets with the rosy-red apples. The farmer went purple with rage, but he couldn't do anything about it. He didn't want to break his leg by jumping down to the ground.

Meddle trotted off down to the village. He met Mr Jinky and spoke to him.

'Where's the fire?'

'What fire?' said Jinky.

'The house on fire. I'm going to rescue somebody with this ladder,' said Meddle. 'You know – climb up to a top window.'

'Oh,' said Jinky. 'Well, I should find the fire first if I were you.'

Meddle thought that was a silly remark. He went on his way, looking for the fire. But nobody's house seemed to be on fire. He could still see the spire of smoke rising up in the air, so he went towards it as fast as he could, carrying the heavy ladder over his shoulder.

'Where are you going with that ladder?' asked Dame Trot-About in surprise, when he nearly knocked her over with one end of it.

'Just off to rescue somebody from the burning house!' said Meddle importantly. 'Out of my way, please!'

'What burning house?' asked Dame Trot-About in surprise. But Meddle had gone round the corner, almost knocking down a lamp-post with the long ladder!

At last he came to where the smoke rose high in the air. But oh, what a dreadful disappointment for poor Meddle, it was only the smoke from Mr Smiley's garden bonfire. It was a very, very good bonfire, and the smoke rose high from it. Mr Smiley was piling all kinds of things on it to make it burn well.

'So there isn't a house on fire after all, and there isn't anyone to rescue!' said poor Meddle sadly. Mr Smiley thought Meddle must be mad.

'I don't know what you mean,' he said. 'Why are you taking that heavy ladder about?'

Meddle didn't answer. He turned sadly round, almost knocking one of Mr Smiley's trees down with the end of the ladder, and went back to Farmer Corny's orchard.

As soon as he got there he heard the farmer's angry voice. 'You wait till I catch you young monkeys! Stealing my apples like that! You just wait!'

The naughty boys didn't see Meddle coming back with the ladder. Meddle saw at once what had happened, and he put the ladder back up the farmer's tree. Farmer Corny was down in a second.

Didn't those bad boys get a shock! My goodness me, there was the farmer at the bottom of their tree. And what a scolding they got when they came down. They had to empty their pockets of the apples and off they went howling.

Then the farmer turned to Meddle, who was standing near by watching. 'Good thing I brought the ladder back when I did,' said Meddle, thinking that he had done the farmer a good turn.

'What did you want to take it away for?' cried the farmer, and to Meddle's enormous surprise, he found himself caught by the farmer's huge hand and shaken hard – so hard that his teeth rattled in his head, and he was afraid they would fall out!

'*I'll* teach you to take ladders to rescue

people!' cried the farmer. '*I'll* teach you to let bad boys get into my trees and steal my apples. *I'll* teach you to leave me stuck up a tree for ages!'

He did teach Meddle – for I'm sure he will never, never take a ladder again and go rushing off to rescue people from a burning house that is only a bonfire.

Poor old Meddle!

Chapter 11

Mister Meddle is Rather Foolish

Once upon a time Mister Meddle went on a walking tour with Mr Jinks, his friend. They walked all day long in the summer heat, and got rather tired and very hot and extremely cross.

And then Mr Jinks began to sneeze! Mister Meddle stared at him in amazement.

'Jinks! You don't mean to say you can possibly have caught cold in this hot weather?'

'Well, that's just when you *do* catch cold!' said Jinks, blowing his nose. 'You get very hot – and then take off a lot of clothes – and the wind blows, and hey presto – atishoo – a cold has arrived!'

'How very silly!' said Mister Meddle. 'Well, come on, Jinks. We'll never get to the next village if we don't hurry! I want something to eat – and then we'll go to bed, bed, bed, and rest our poor tired feet.'

'It's a pity we have to use our feet so much on a walking holiday,' groaned Mr Jinks. 'I should enjoy walking so much more if I could go on a bicycle.'

'Don't be silly,' said Meddle.

'That's twice you've said I'm silly,' said Jinks crossly. I wish you'd be quiet if you can't say anything more polite.'

'All right,' said Meddle. 'I won't say another word!'

And he didn't, not even when Jinks asked him a question. So by the time they arrived at the next village and looked for an inn they were not the best of friends.

They found a cosy, little inn and went inside. They had a fine supper of ham and eggs, stewed plums, custard and cocoa. After that they both felt so sleepy that they fell asleep in their chairs and didn't wake up till it was dark.

'This *is* silly of us!' groaned Jinks, waking up and yawning. 'Come on, Meddle, let's go to bed. A-tish-oo! A-TISH-OO! Oh, bother this cold!'

'I hope you keep it to yourself and don't give it to me,' said Meddle. 'Hurry up. I've lit the candle.'

They both went upstairs. They had a cosy bedroom with a funny slanting ceiling and a floor that went up and down, it was so uneven.

They undressed and got into bed. 'Isn't it hot?' said Meddle. 'We'd better open the window.'

'Oh no, please don't,' said Jinks, sneezing again. 'I shall get a much worse cold if we have an open window with the wind blowing on us all night long.'

'But, Jinks, I can't sleep if I'm hot,' said Meddle.

'And I can't sleep if I'm cold,' said Jinks firmly. 'And what's more, I'm JOLLY WELL NOT going to have the window open tonight. Do you want me to be too ill in the morning to go on with our walking?'

'Oh, well, please yourself,' said Meddle, getting into bed. 'But I tell you this, Jinks, I am QUITE, QUITE SURE that I shan't be able to go to sleep unless the window is open.'

They both shut their eyes. Jinks sneezed and coughed. Meddle tossed and turned. He felt hotter and hotter and hotter. It was dreadful! Oh, to have the window open and feel a nice cool breeze blowing! He could go to sleep at once then.

'I'm so dreadfully hot,' said Meddle. He breathed very fast to show Jinks how hot he was. 'I almost feel that my tongue will hang out like a dog's soon.'

'Well, if it does, perhaps you'll stop talking

and let *me* get to sleep,' said Jinks crossly.

'Jinks! How perfectly horrid you are!' cried Meddle. 'Oh dear! I'm so hot I must throw all the clothes off.'

'Well, don't throw them off me, too!' said Jinks, clutching at the blankets as Meddle threw them off. 'Oh, do lie down and go to sleep. You're just making a fuss. I could easily go to sleep if only you would.'

'Well, I tell you that I shall never, never, never go to sleep if we don't have the window open,' groaned Meddle.

'Oh, for goodness' sake, open it then,' said Jinks crossly. '*I'll* never go to sleep as long as you lie awake throwing all the clothes off me, and tossing about like a whale trying to catch its dinner.'

'Don't be silly,' said Meddle.

'That's the third time you've said that,' said Jinks fiercely, sitting up in bed. 'If you say it again I'll throw you out of bed.'

'All right, all right,' said Meddle, getting out of bed. 'I'm going to open the window. Wherever is it?'

'Over there,' said Jinks.

'What do you mean, over there?' said Meddle, feeling around. 'There's an awful lot of over theres in this room. But there doesn't seem to be any window.'

'Of course there is,' said Jinks. 'Light the candle and find it.'

'The candle seems to have disappeared, and the matches, too,' said Meddle, feeling about. 'Ah – I believe I've got the window now, I can feel glass!'

'I'm sure the window wasn't there,' said Jinks, in surprise. 'I thought there was a bookcase there or a ta le or something.'

'Well, you thought wrong,' said Meddle, fumbling round the glass. 'A window is made of glass, isn't it? Well, this is glass, so it's the window. Don't be silly.'

'Meddle! I'll kick you out of bed as soon as you get in!' said Jinks furiously.

'Don't worry. I shan't be in for a long, long time yet,' said Meddle dolefully. 'I can't seem to find out how to open this silly window at all. It just doesn't seem to open at the top or bottom or the side. Oh, I'm getting so ANGRY with it!'

'Tell it not to be silly,' said Jinks.

'Well, I will!' said Meddle, and he spoke angrily to the window. 'Don't be silly, window! If you don't let me open you, I'll smash you and let the fresh air in that way!'

But it was no good. Meddle simply could *not* open the window at all. He got angrier and angrier. And to make things worse, Jinks suddenly began to giggle. How he giggled! He went on and on like a river running down hill. Meddle was simply furious with him.

'Now what in the wide world are you giggling about, Jinks?' he said. 'Is it so funny that I can't open the window?'

'Yes, Meddle – if you only knew what I know, you'd be giggling, too!' chuckled Jinks, stuffing the sheet into his mouth to stop himself from laughing.

'Well, what *do* you know,' said Meddle, slapping his hand against the glass angrily.'

'Shan't tell you,' said Jinks. 'You keep calling me silly – so I'll be silly and not tell you.'

'Well, you're sillier than I even thought you were,' said Meddle in disgust. 'Oh, you awful window! Oh, you horrid thing! Take that – and that – and that!'

Meddle hit out for all he was worth – and there came the sound of breaking glass!

'Ah!' said Meddle. 'I'm glad I've broken you, very glad. You deserved it. Now the fresh

air can come in and I can breathe it and go to sleep. Ahhhh – the lovely fresh air!'

Meddle sniffed and sniffed, thinking how marvellously cool the room had become.

'Don't you feel the lovely fresh air blowing in, Jinks?' he asked.

'No, I don't,' said Jinks.

'What! Can't you feel the cool breeze?' cried Meddle, climbing into bed.

'No, I can't,' said Jinks, and he gave another giggle.

'I simply don't know what's come over you tonight, Jinks,' said Meddle, settling down under the blankets. 'Giggling like that over nothing. You ought to be ashamed of yourself.'

'*You'll* be ashamed of yourself in the morning,' said Jinks, with another helpless giggle.

'I certainly shan't,' said Meddle. 'My word, it's quite cool now that I've broken that window and let in the cold night air. Good night, Jinks, I hope you'll have got over your giggles by the morning.'

Jinks had another fit of giggles, and shook the bed with them. Meddle shut is eyes and was soon asleep. And then Jinks slept too, though once he awoke and began to giggle again.

In the morning Meddle sat up and yawned. He stared at the window. It was fast shut! The glass was not broken at all!

'There's a funny thing!' said Meddle. 'Didn't I break you last night, window?'

Jinks sat up and began to giggle again. He pointed to a bookcase over in the corner. It had a glass front to it that was locked – and some of the glass was smashed!

'Oh, Meddle! You broke that glass-fronted bookcase last night and not the window!' said

Jinks, going off into a laugh. 'I knew you had – that's why I began to giggle. It was so funny the way you kept asking me if I didn't feel the cool air coming in through the broken window – and all the time the window was quite whole and fast shut, and it was the bookcase you had broken!'

'Goodness gracious!' said Meddle, in dismay. 'I'll have to pay a lot of money for that. Well, well – how was it I thought I felt the cold night air coming in, I wonder? I just simply can't understand it!'

'I can!' said Jinks, going off into giggles again. 'You're just a silly, Meddle – just a GREAT BIG SILLY!'

And for once poor Meddle couldn't find any answer at all!

Chapter 12

Mister Meddle and the Horse

Now once Farmer Straw was ill, and he was worried about his horse.

'He needs someone to look after him,' he said to his servant, Annie. 'Send for Meddle. Maybe he can keep an eye on him for me. He will need feeding, and watering, and a little canter over the hills now and again.'

So Meddle was sent for and Farmer Straw told him about the horse.

'You keep an eye on him for me,' he said. 'He is a good, well-mannered horse, and won't be any trouble. He is a wise old fellow, is Captain, and he understands every word you say to him.'

'Does he really?' said Meddle, surprised. 'Well, I shan't have much difficulty with him, then. Don't you worry, Farmer Straw, Captain and I will get on well together.'

'There are oats in the bin,' said the farmer. 'And the grooming-brush is in his stable. You'll have to give him water, too, because the field he is in has no stream running through it.'

'Right,' said Meddle, and walked off, feeling most important. He had once looked after a canary, and once looked after his aunt's cat – but he had never looked after such a big animal as a horse before.

'Such a wise old horse, too,' thought Meddle. 'Understands every word said to him. Fancy that! Well, I can ask him what he wants, and he'll know all right.'

Meddle went to the field where Captain was. The horse cantered over to him.

'Hello, Captain,' said Meddle, and patted his nose. 'Do you want a nice drink of water? I can bring you some in a pail, if you do.'

'Nay-ay-ay-ay-ay?' neighed the horse, pleased to hear the word 'water' for he was thirsty.

'Nay?' said Meddle. 'Did you say "nay"? That means no. So you don't want any water. All right. You really are a clever horse. You not only understand what I say to you, but you answer, too.'

Meddle went off to get his dinner. The horse looked after him, disappointed. He wanted some water, but he didn't get it.

After dinner Meddle went back to the horse, which cantered eagerly to the gate.

'Would you like some oats?' asked Meddle.

'Nay-ay-ay-ay-ay!' neighed the horse, in delight. Oats! Just what he would like! The grass in his field was very poor – but oats were good.

'Nay?' said Meddle, surprised. 'Dear me –

fancy not wanting oats. I shouldn't have thought a big hefty horse like you would have said "nay" to oats. I should have thought you would have said "yes".'

He looked at the horse, who nuzzled against him, trying to let him know that he wanted both oats and water. Meddle stroked his soft nose.

'Would you like to come out of your field for a nice little canter?' he said. 'Farmer Straw said you might like a run over the hills.'

'Nay-ay-ay-ay-ay!' neighed the horse at once in delight. Ah – if he could only get out for a canter, he could drink from the first stream he came to. That would be fine.

'What a horse you are for saying no to everything,' said Meddle. 'Don't you want anything at all, Captain? It's no trouble to me to get you anything you want, you know.'

'Nay-ay-ay-ay-ay,' said the old horse.

'All right,' said Meddle. 'If you don't want anything, I won't get it. I'm off to market now. If you're a good horse, maybe I'll bring you back something you'll like.'

He set off for market. He bought all kinds of things there for himself – and he bought a beautiful bunch of early carrots for Captain,

109

the horse. They were very dear, very small, but very sweet.

'Aha! Captain will like these,' thought Meddle to himself. 'He won't say no to these. He'll say "yes-es-es-es-esssss!"'

He went home with his goods. Then he went to the field, carrying behind him the bunch of feather carrots. He spoke to Captain, who nuzzled at him eagerly, smelling the carrots that Meddle hid behind his back.

'Captain, do you want some nice young carrots?' asked Meddle. 'Now, think before you answer!'

'Nay-ay-ay-ay-ay!' neighed the horse in delight. Carrots! How wonderful. But Meddle was cross.

'There you go – saying no to me again!' he said, angrily. 'What a particular horse you are! Nothing I offer you pleases you! You won't have water, oats, a canter or even new carrots! I am disgusted with you. It's nay, nay, nay all the time. Why don't you say yes, yes, yes, for a change?'

He left the poor, hungry, thirsty old horse and went off home. On the way he passed the farmhouse, and the servant saw him. 'Come

in and speak to the master for a minute,' she said. 'He's fretting about his old horse.'

Meddle marched in. The farmer looked at him. 'Meddle, have you fed and watered my horse? Have you taken him for a canter?'

'No,' said Meddle. 'He's a most obstinate horse. He says "nay-nay-nay" to everything I ask him. What's the use of looking after a horse that says no to everything?'

'Meddle, don't you know a horse can only say "nay"?' cried the farmer. 'Are you cruel, or just stupid? Meddle, come here. I think you need a really good scolding. Come here.'

'Nay-ay-ay-ay-ay!' cried Meddle, and you should have seen him run. He went even faster than the old horse. What a silly he is, isn't he?